the
HICCUPotamus

This book is for Amity
(who makes my heart bam-bamity)

the HICCUPotamus

HIC

by AARON ZENZ

SCHOLASTIC INC.

New York Toronto London Auckland Sydney
Mexico City New Delhi Hong Kong Buenos Aires

Hic!

Hic!

HIC

There was a hippopotamus
Who hiccupped quite-a-lotamus.
And every time he got'emus . . .

. . . He'd fall upon his bottomus.

One day he saw an elephant
With cakes of green and yellowphant.

He tried to tell her "hellophant". . .

. . . But it didn't go so wellephant.

She chased him toward a centipede
Pouring new cementipede.

He hic'ed by accidentipede . . .

. . . And tripped the elephantipede.

They ran near a rhinoceros
With minty dental flosserous.

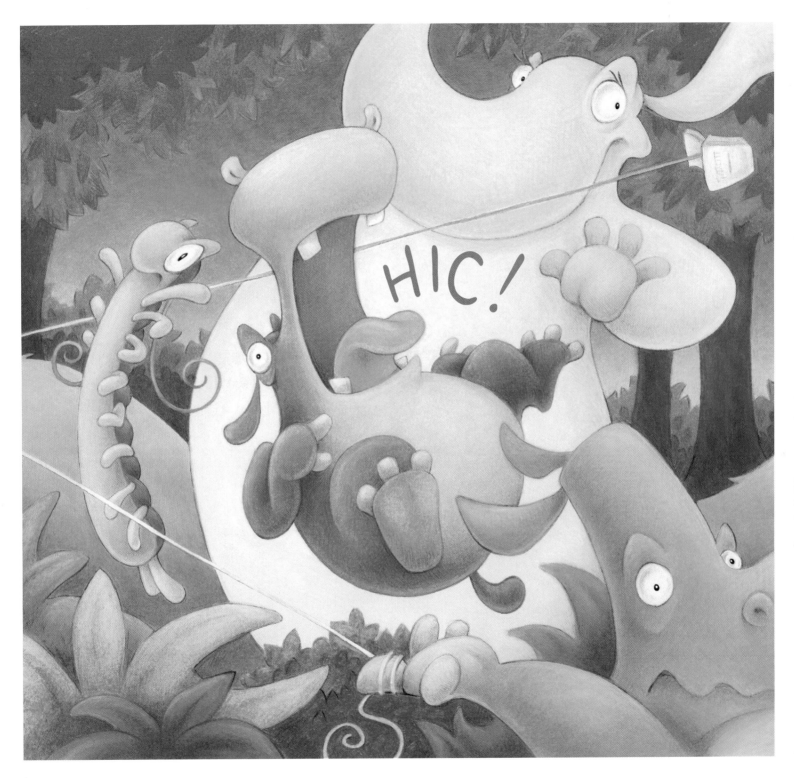

His string went all criss-crosserous . . .

. . . And *that* was the last strawcerous.

They tried to find a therapy –
Some cure which they could shareapy,
A what or why or whereapy
To stop this long nightmareapy.

So . . .

They wrapped him 'round with licorice
And spun him very quickerish.

Puff Puff Puff

They secured him to a buffalo
And made him huff and puffalo.

HIC!

They acquired an aquarium
And flashed him something scaryum.

They poured him tubs of vinegar
And tickled his chinny-chin-chinigar.

HIC!

And then at last – a miracle!
His hiccups, so severeacle,
Just didn't reappearacle!
He grinned from ear to earacle.

Until . . .

ISBN-13: 978-0-439-89781-5
ISBN-10: 0-439-89781-5

12 11 10 9 8 7 6 5 4 3 2 1   7 8 9 10 11/0

Printed in the U.S.A.   40

First Scholastic printing, September 2006

The artwork was created entirely in colored pencil.

No actual licorice was misused in the making of this book.

Cast Bios

The part of the Hiccupotamus was played by veteran hippo actor Hank Polowski. Due to a paralyzing fear of fish, some of his scenes in this book were performed by a crew of stunt doubles.

Bartholomew Poppins has appeared in over 100 roles in his picture book career. He still dreams of landing a leading part, but is proud of his work in *The Hiccupotamus* and his cameo as "something squishy" in *Mr. Binkers Steps in Something Squishy*.

Many considered it a risk casting an unknown in the significant elephant role. But it would appear that pachyderm Katie McMurphy has a promising career ahead of her. Following a serious allergic reaction, however, she is currently turning down all parts that involve the use of frosting.

Samu Ti speaks no English, which created occasional confusion during his work on *The Hiccupotamus*. Author Aaron Zenz recalls the time the script called for the centipede to pour cement, but instead Samu began purring like a cat. "The more I shouted 'Pour! Pour!' the louder he'd purr!"

This is the final role for Dennis Flott. He is retiring to a small beekeeping community in North Western Idaho. Good luck, Dennis! We wish you all the best.

The part of the buffalo was played by a groundsquirrel named Arlo. It took 14 hours in the make-up chair to get him ready each day. Unfortunately, that continually made for a very short window of opportunity to use him in costume.